The Twelve Days of Christmas

SUSAN JEFFERS

HARPER

An Imprint of HarperCollinsPublishers

ON CHRISTMAS EVE, when

everyone was sleeping, I tiptoed to the closet and found

a present from Santa.

When I opened the box, music began to play.

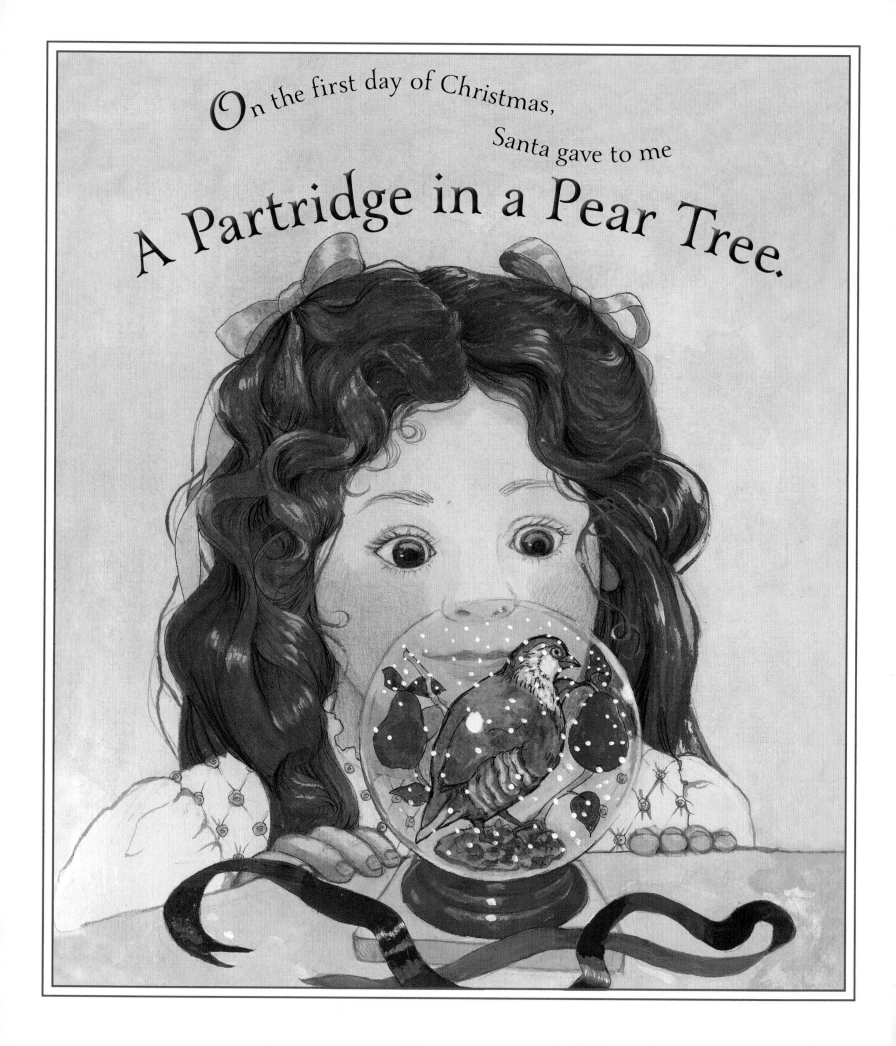

On the second day of Christmas,

Santa gave to me

Two Turtledoves.

On the third day of Christmas,
Santa gave to me

Three French Hens.

On the fourth day of Christmas,
Santa gave to me

Four Calling Birds.

On the fifth day of Christmas,
Santa gave to me

Five Golden Rings.

On the sixth day of Christmas,
Santa gave to me

Six Geese A'laying.

On the seventh day of Christmas,
Santa gave to me

Seven Swans A'swimming.

On the eighth day of Christmas,
Santa gave to me

Eight Maids A'milking.

On the ninth day of Christmas,

Santa gave to me

Nine Ladies
Dancing.

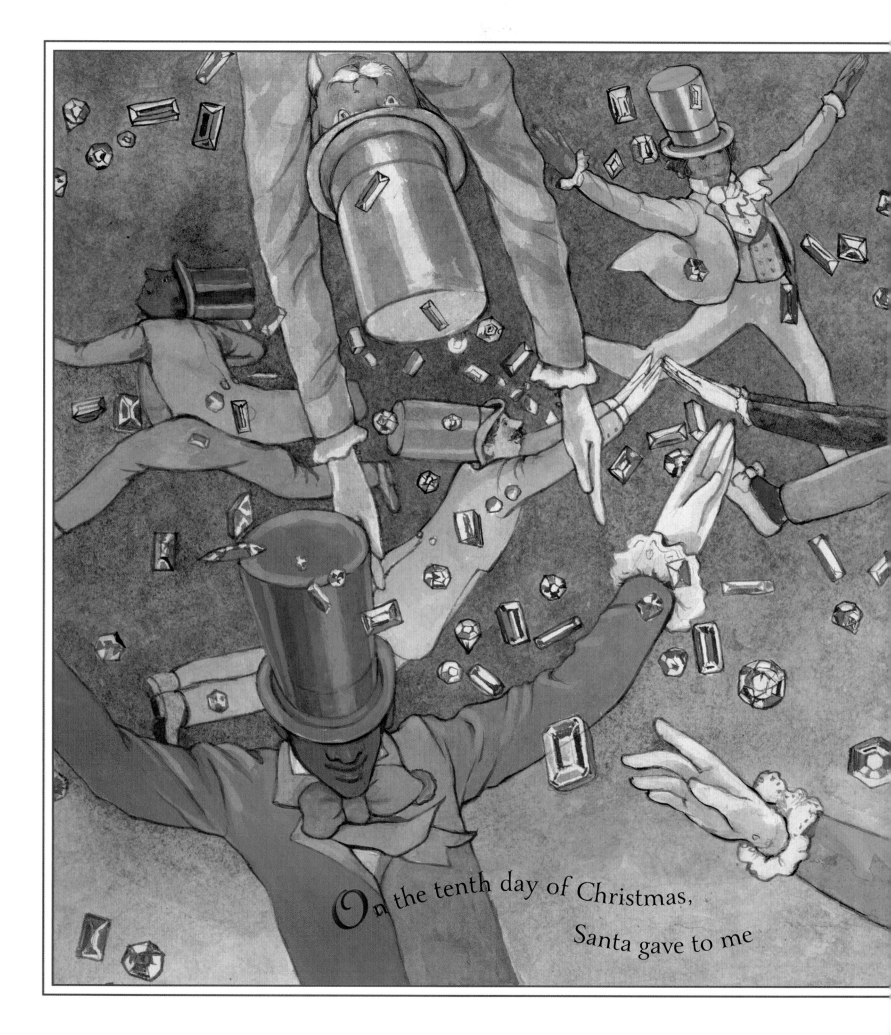

On the tenth day of Christmas,

Santa gave to me

Ten Lords A'leaping.

On the eleventh day of Christmas,
Santa gave to me

Eleven Drummers Drumming.

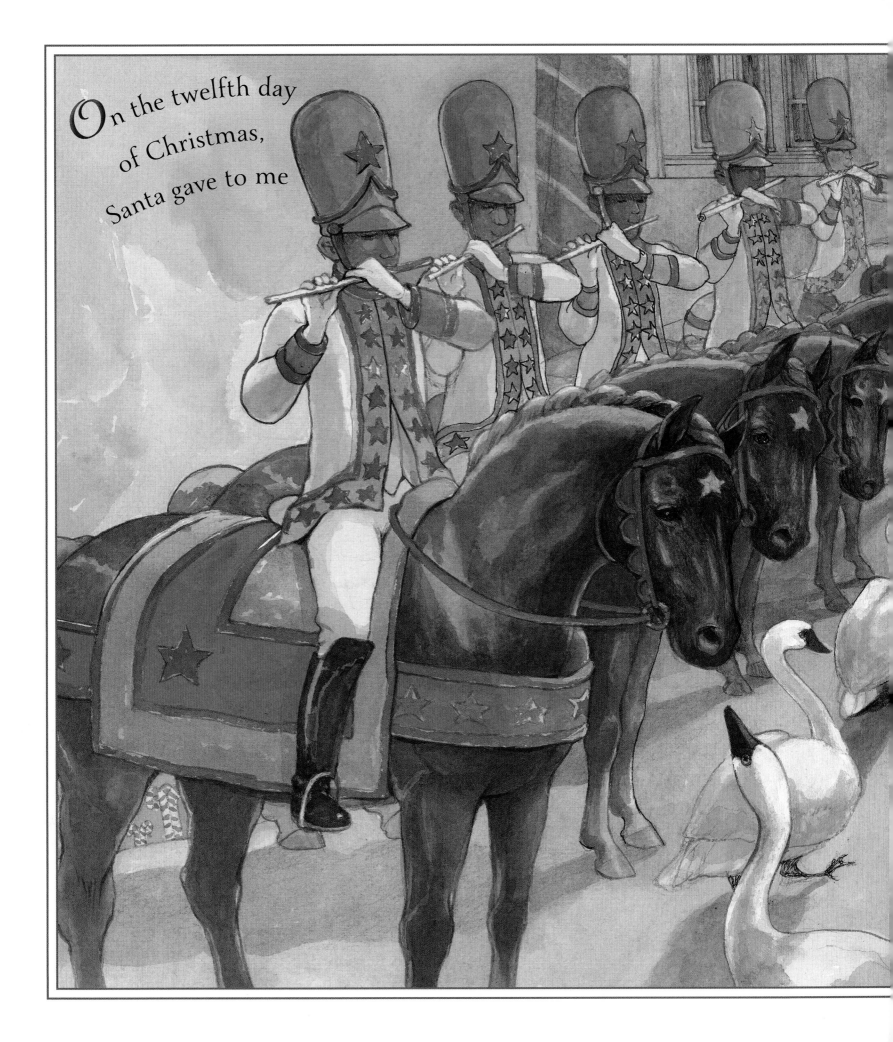

On the twelfth day
of Christmas,
Santa gave to me

Twelve Pipers Piping.

The Pipers piped us right up to Santa's front door.

Inside Santa's workshop I saw
more toys than I'd ever seen before!

Then Santa smiled and said, "Emma, I think you have something to show me."

I handed Santa my
broken toy, climbed
up into his big
armchair . . .

. . . and dreamed that reindeer
were flying us through the air.

On Christmas morning,

I raced down the stairs . . .

. . . to see

my Partridge in a Pear Tree!

For Sharon Lerner, who helped make this book a reality.
Sharon, my cherished friend, with her high spirits, thoughtful suggestions,
and gentle understanding of the child's heart, brought this Twelve Days of Christmas *to life.*
It is no surprise that Sharon is a longtime editor, author, and producer of children's media
and a member of the founding team of Sesame Street, *the most beloved children's program of all time.*

Notes

One of the most engaging things about being an illustrator of children's books is the opportunity to create my drawings of the iconic figures in children's literature, such as Cinderella, Thumbelina, the Nutcracker—and now, the Three French Hens!

When I was a child, I began to imagine drawings in the church choir loft while I waited to sing. When the sermons got a bit slow, I would dream up scenes from my favorite stories to keep myself from fidgeting. I'd picture how I would show the characters moving about in their dramatic situations. In my mind I would draw the Snow Queen and her flying sled, Black Beauty running across the fields, Cinderella, Thumbelina, and many others. Unbeknownst to me, I was developing the technique I would use when I became a professional artist. When I decided I wanted to do a version of *The Twelve Days of Christmas* that would appeal to children, I entertained various notions of how all of the extraordinary gifts could be portrayed in a lively story. After I talked things over with my friend Sharon Lerner, whose idea of a trip to Santa's workshop, accompanied by ladies dancing and lords a'leaping, helped the story take shape, I began sketching scenes that would be used in the book.

When drawing people, I always use real-life models for inspiration. For this particular story, Sasha Nelson was my Emma, her dad, Josh Nelson, made a good Santa, and Elaine Llewellyn helped. My daughter, Ali Phillips, and her husband, Chad Phillips, directed the models and photographed the scenes. Using these as a reference, I again began sketching. Many drawings (and much counting of characters) later, I turned to my favorite 350-pound watercolor paper and began to paint, hoping that children would enjoy this whimsical interpretation of a holiday favorite.

Library of Congress Cataloging-in-Publication Data is available. ISBN 978-0-06-206615-2 (trade bdg.) – ISBN 978-0-06-206616-9 (lib. bdg.)

The artist used watercolor and ink on Arches watercolor paper to create the illustrations for this book. Typography by Martha Rago.

13 14 15 16 17 SCP 10 9 8 7 6 5 4 3 2 1 ❖ First Edition